GIRLS ROCK

Girl Pirat

illustrated by
Meredith Thomas

First published in Great Britain by
RISING STARS UK LTD 2005
76 Farnaby Road, Bromley, BR1 4BH

Reprinted 2006 (twice)

For information visit our website at:
www.risingstars-uk.com

British Library Cataloguing in Publication Data

A CIP record for this book is available from the British Library.

ISBN: 1-905056-19-2

First published in 2005 by
MACMILLAN EDUCATION AUSTRALIA PTY LTD
627 Chapel Street, South Yarra, Australia 3141

Visit our website at www.macmillan.com.au

Associated companies and representatives throughout the world.

Series created by Felice Arena and Phil Kettle
Project Management by Limelight Press Pty Ltd
Cover and text design by Lore Foye
Illustrations by Meredith Thomas

Printed and bound in Great Britain by
Mackays of Chatham plc, Chatham, Kent

GIRLS ROCK!
Contents

Mai   Carly

CHAPTER 1

Up, Up and Away

Best friends Carly and Mai are
in Carly's garden, playing on
the trampoline.

Mai "This is really cool. Trampolining is the best fun. I feel like I'm flying!"

Carly "Yes it beats hanging about inside."

The girls jump high enough to see over the fence into the neighbour's garden.

Mai "Hey, Joey and Tom look like they're playing pirates."

Carly "They don't look much like pirates to me. They wouldn't scare off too many sailors in those trousers."

The girls slow down their jumping so they can get a better look at the boys next door.

Mai "And what about the paper swords—pretty useless if you ask me."

Carly "They're ridiculous. I'd never give over my treasure to them. They just look so stupid."

Mai "We'd make better pirates any day."

Carly "Definitely, we could launch an attack with real style."

The girls start to hatch a plan.

Carly "Why don't we give them a real run for their money? Girl pirates, here we come!"

Mai "Great idea! We'll need to look the part, though."

Carly "I'm sure my mum will have loads of pirate gear inside."

Mai "We'll plan the best pirate attack in history. Those boys won't know what's hit them."

Carly (laughing quietly) "No, especially when *we've* finished with them!"

The girls climb down off the trampoline.

CHAPTER 2

Setting Sail

Carly and Mai head inside to Carly's mum's wardrobe, in search of pirate clothes.

Mai "These baggy trousers and big shirts are perfect."

Carly "Put these earrings on."

Mai "Won't your mum freak if she sees us wearing these?"

Carly "We can put them back when we've finished—she'll never know."

Carly and Mai find all sorts of bits and pieces to make the perfect pirate outfits.

Carly "We make much better pirates than they do."

Mai "Agreed, we're the meanest pirates that have ever sailed the seas."

Carly "And the smartest."

Mai "But we're missing one thing."

Carly "What?"

Mai "A boat."

Carly "Pirates have ships. They don't have boats."

Mai "Boat ... ship ... whatever. We just need something we can be pirates in!"

Carly "How about the trampoline?"

Mai "OK, cool. We can tie brushes and rakes at each corner then drape a sheet across the tree to make a sail."

Carly "Great idea! And when we move on the trampoline it'll be just like we're on the high seas."

The girls start putting their ship together and before long it's ready to sail.

Mai "All we need now is food, weapons and bombs."

Carly "Yes, then we'll be ready to attack, and to raid their treasure."

Mai "We'll capture the boy pirates and tie them up."

Carly "And then we can make them our slaves!"

Mai "They couldn't survive as our slaves. They'll soon tell us where they've buried their treasure."

Carly "Just think, we'll have everything we need from those hopeless boy pirates."

The girls fall down on the trampoline, laughing hysterically.

CHAPTER 3

Perfume Bombs

Carly and Mai go back inside. They fill a basket with food, then get what they need to make water bombs for their pirate adventure.

Carly "We need to make the best bombs ever."

Mai "Yes, the bombs need to destroy the boy pirates forever!"
Carly "Then we'll win the battle!"

Carly starts to fill up balloons with water.

Mai "These bombs are kind of boring. We need something better."

Carly "Ahh, well I've got a plan. Our bombs will be more powerful than any other bomb ever made. You'll see."

Carly goes back into her mother's bedroom. She returns carrying a bottle.

Mai "Isn't that your mother's favourite perfume?"

Carly "Yes, but if we only put a few drops in each bomb, it'll totally destroy the boy pirates. It's our secret weapon!"

Mai (laughing) "They'll all smell like our mothers, and that'll make them die."

The girls put a bit of perfume in each water bomb and soon the bottle is empty.

Mai "What'll we tell your mother?"
Carly "Let's just fill it up with water and put it back. Mum will never know."

The girls put the bottle back and
go outside. They load all their food
and weapons onto their ship.

Mai "We're ready to sail."

Carly "I want to be Captain Cut Throat."

Mai "Well I'll be Captain Throat Cut."

Carly "Great idea! We'll be the best and fiercest girl pirates ever!"

CHAPTER 4

Water War

The girls board their ship.

Mai "Time to venture into the wild seas."

Carly "Now for some serious pirating!"

The girls look over the fence again.

Carly "We'd better keep a look out for other pirates."

Mai "You never know where they might be. These seas are full of surprises."

Carly "We'll probably smell them
before we see them."

Mai "I think I can hear them now."

Carly "I think I can *smell* them now."

Mai "Prepare to attack!"

Just as the girls are ready, a water
bomb appears from nowhere and
explodes on the deck of the ship.

Carly "We're under attack!"

Mai "Look out or we'll get hit."

The girls put up two umbrellas, as quick as a flash.

Mai "I bet the boy pirates don't have good protection like us."

Carly "Of course they won't! They're not as smart as us."

Mai "Ready? Bombs away!"

Moments later, groans come from next door. The boys have been hit. This is now a major sea battle.

Carly "I guess they'll surrender."

Mai "They might want to but do we want to let them?"

Carly "No way! I don't want to go easy on them."

Mai "Yes, they started it. We'll fight to the finish."

CHAPTER 5

And the Winners Are?

The girls keep tossing bombs over
the fence at the boy pirates. Sounds
of "They got me!", "Ah gross!", "What
is that?", "You stink!", "So do you!"
and "Yuk!" can be heard as the
bombs burst all over the boys.

Carly "Look, there's a white flag."
Mai "I think that means they've given up."

The boys yell out from the deck of their ship, "We give up! We give up! Your bombs made us stink like our mothers. Gross!"

Carly "We're the best pirates ever."
Mai "And the smartest!"

The girls start doing a victory
dance but stop when they catch
sight of Carly's mother looking really
cross and holding a perfume bottle.

Mai (under her breath) "Uh-oh. This doesn't look good."

Carly "You can say that again. There's only one thing scarier than pirates."

Mai "What?"

Carly "My mum when she's angry.
Prepare to surrender, Captain."

Mai "Aye-aye Captain. I'm ready to
go down with the ship."

Carly "Good, because we're in big
trouble!"

GIRLS ROCK!

Girl Pirate Lingo

Mai

Carly

bow This is the pointed end of a boat. Or it can be what boys should do when they talk to girls.

boy attack! What girls say when they are ready to throw water bombs at boys.

man overboard What you should yell out when someone has fallen overboard. Hopefully it's a boy, which means one less of them—and that's good!

port The left side of the boat as you face the bow. Starboard is what you call the right side of the boat.

stern This is the back or the big end of the boat.

GIRLS ROCK!
Girl Pirate Must-dos

☆ Pull up the anchor before you try to make the boat move.

☆ Make sure that you have a plank on your boat. You never know when you might need to make some boys walk the plank.

☆ Carry water bombs with perfume in them. This is the best defence against boys.

☆ Make sure that you take a compass on your pirate trips so you don't get lost!

☆ Learn to yell "Girls Rock!" really loud.

☆ Make sure that you take plenty of yummy food on board your ship. You could be at sea for a long time.

☆ Draw a map to show where you have hidden your treasure.

☆ Ask your mother before you use any of her clothes ... or her perfume!

GIRLS ROCK!
Girl Pirate Instant Info

 Pirates always fly a flag when they are about to attack another ship.

 A pirate's flag has a skull and crossbones on it.

 According to historical records, the most famous female pirates were two women by the names of Anne Bonny and Mary Reid.

 One of the most famous pirates of all time was Blackbeard. His real name was Edward Teach.

In the classic story of *Peter Pan*, Peter's main enemy was an evil pirate by the name of Captain Hook.

 "Pirates of the Caribbean" is a Disneyland theme-park ride and also a blockbuster movie starring Johnny Depp and Geoffrey Rush.

If you have "sea legs", you are able to walk steadily on a ship that is rolling on high seas, and you don't get seasick.

Think Tank

1 Who were the most famous girl pirates?

2 What's usually on a pirate flag?

3 What do female pirates hunt for?

4 What does "Aye, aye, captain!" mean?

5 What should you wear when you are on a boat or ship?

6 If the Captain says "Get to the port side", what side of the ship should you go to?

7 What do you call the pointed end of a ship?

8 What sort of ship has a mast?

Answers

8 Sailing ships or yachts have a mast which sails are attached to.

7 The pointed end of a ship is called the bow.

6 The port side is the left side of the ship as you face the pointed end.

5 You should always wear a life jacket on a boat or ship.

4 This expression is the pirate's way of saying "yes sir".

3 Female pirates, like all pirates, like to hunt for treasure.

2 A skull and cross bones are usually on a pirate flag.

1 The most famous female pirates were Anne Bonny and Mary Reid. (But Carly and Mai are pretty famous, too!)

How did you score?

- If you got 8 answers correct, you're a natural girl pirate and you could end up sailing the high seas!

- If you got 6 answers correct, you have the makings of a great girl pirate but you probably prefer to sail on calm seas.

- If you got fewer than 4 answers correct, you may not have sea legs but you're the perfect person to guard the treasure on land.

Hey Girls!

I hope that you have as much fun reading my story as I have had writing it.

I loved reading and writing stories when I was young.

Try some of these suggestions to make reading even more fun.

At school, why don't you use "Girl Pirates" as a play? You and your friends can be the actors.

Make a pirate flag and a map to use as props. Make sure that you leave your water bombs at home or you might get into trouble! You can pretend that you and your friends are about to attack a "Boy Pirate Ship".

So ... have you decided who is going to be Mai and who is going to be Carly? Now, with your friends, read and act out this play in front of your classmates. It will definitely make the whole class laugh.

You can also take the story home and get someone to act out the parts with you.

So, get ready to have more fun with your reading than Santa has on Christmas Eve!

And remember, Girls Rock!

Sheykettle.

GIRLS ROCK!
When We Were Kids

Shey

Jacqueline

Shey talked to Jacqueline, another
Girls Rock! author.

Shey "Have you ever gone sailing?"

Jacqueline "Yes, I used to sail with my
friend out in the harbour."

Shey "Really? Was it like being on the
high seas?"

Jacqueline "Sometimes, especially
when the wind was really blowing."

Shey "Were you ever attacked by
pirates?"

Jacqueline "No, but I wish I had been."

Shey "Why?"

Jacqueline "Because then Johnny
Depp could have rescued me, like
in 'Pirates of the Caribbean'!"

GIRLS ROCK!
What a Laugh!

Q What's a girl pirate's favourite letter of the alphabet?

A C!

GIRLS ROCK!

Read about the fun
that girls have in these
GIRLS ROCK! titles:

The Sleepover

Pool Pals

Bowling Buddies

Girl Pirates

Netball Showdown

School Play Stars

Diary Disaster

Horsing Around

GIRLS ROCK! books are available from
most booksellers. For mail order information
please call Rising Stars on 01933 443862 or visit
www.risingstars-uk.com